Dragon Dancing

by Carole Lexa Schaefer

illustrated by

Pierr Morgan

Viking

At school, our teacher reads to us—
a book about dragons.

After, in the art room,

we decorate for Mei Lin's birthday

with sparkly paper and ribbons.

Snip, *twirl*, flip.

"Look at *me*!" Mei Lin shouts.

"I'm *Birthday* Dragon!"

"You need some boink-boink eyes," says Willy.

"And—*fa-foom!*" shouts Juan.
"A dragon-fire nose."

"Dragons have ricky-rack backs,"

Emma tells us.

"And long, long, long tails," says Tyrone.

"With feathers," says Jo-Jo.

"And spangles and scales," I say.

We add things on, and add things on,

until . . .

. . . the sparkle-head dragon roars,
"Let's go *Dragon Dancing!*"

Then all of us—in a long dragon line—

go **stomp, bomp-tromping** away . . .

. . . out the **whish-whoosh** doors.

Zig-zagging

over snowy mountaintops.

Slip-sliding

across foamy seas.

Creep-crouching through tall forests.

Mish-mooshing along soft marshes.

Swirl-whirling around whispery meadows.

La-dee-daw-dawdling

under sweet cherry

blossom trees

until . . .

. . . from far, far away,

we hear our teacher calling.

Stomp. Tromp. Ker-bomp.

We are back, for . . .

. . . Birthday Dragon's *SNACK*!

"Grr-umble-yumble-YUMMM!"

For all the children: past, present, and future—*C.L.S.*

For Cynthia—*P.M.*

VIKING
Published by Penguin Group
Penguin Young Readers Group, 345 Hudson Street, New York, New York 10014, U.S.A.
Penguin Group (Canada), 90 Eglinton Avenue East, Suite 700, Toronto,
Ontario, Canada M4P 2Y3 (a division of Pearson Penguin Canada Inc.)
Penguin Books Ltd, 80 Strand, London WC2R 0RL, England
Penguin Ireland, 25 St Stephen's Green, Dublin 2, Ireland
(a division of Penguin Books Ltd)
Penguin Group (Australia), 250 Camberwell Road, Camberwell, Victoria 3124, Australia
(a division of Pearson Australia Group Pty Ltd)
Penguin Books India Pvt Ltd, 11 Community Centre, Panchsheel Park,
New Delhi – 110 017, India
Penguin Group (NZ), Cnr Airborne and Rosedale Roads, Albany, Auckland 1310,
New Zealand (a division of Pearson New Zealand Ltd)
Penguin Books (South Africa) (Pty) Ltd, 24 Sturdee Avenue,
Rosebank, Johannesburg 2196, South Africa

Penguin Books Ltd, Registered Offices: 80 Strand, London WC2R 0RL, England

1 3 5 7 9 10 8 6 4 2

Text copyright © Carole Lexa Schaefer, 2007
Illustrations copyright © Pierr Morgan, 2007
All rights reserved

LIBRARY OF CONGRESS CATALOGING-IN-PUBLICATION DATA IS AVAILABLE
ISBN: 978-0-670-06084-9

Manufactured in China
Set in Godlike & Calligraphic
Book design by Nancy Brennan